**_Join_ the Ghostwriter Te**

**You How**

- Put together a detective k
- Create lots of secret code
- Discover how to write invisi essages
- Use disguises to track down criminals
- Find, lift, and identify fingerprints
- And more!

**_Read_ the Solve-It-Yourself Mysteries . . .**

Follow the Ghostwriter team and see if *you* can solve:

- The Marathon Mystery Message
- The Case of the Shocking-Pink Envelope
- The Case of the One-Armed Shoplifter

**and**

**_Find_ the Hidden Secret Messages from Ghostwriter That Only _You_ Can Decipher . . .**

- Then use the special decoder wheel you'll find right in this book to answer Ghostwriter's final question on page 75!

## Join the Team!

Do you watch GHOSTWRITER on PBS? Then you know that when you read and write to solve a mystery or unravel a puzzle, you're using the same smarts and skills the Ghostwriter team uses.

We hope you'll join the team and read along to help solve the mysterious and puzzling goings-on in these GHOSTWRITER books!

# DETECTIVE GUIDE

## TOOLS AND TRICKS OF THE TRADE

by

Susan Lurie

Illustrated by Felipe Galindo

A
CHILDREN'S TELEVISION WORKSHOP
BOOK

BANTAM BOOKS
NEW YORK • TORONTO • LONDON • SYDNEY • AUCKLAND

*THE GHOSTWRITER DETECTIVE GUIDE*
*A Bantam Book / November 1992*



*Art direction by Marva Martin*
*Cover photo by Walt Chrynwski*
*Cover design by Susan Herr*
*Interior illustrations by Felipe Galindo*



ISBN 0-553-48069-3

*Published simultaneously in the United States and Canada*

***Bantam Books are published by Bantam Books, a division of Bantam Doubleday Dell Publishing Group, Inc. Its trademark, consisting of the words "Bantam Books" and the portrayal of a rooster, is Registered in U.S. Patent and Trademark Office and in other countries. Marca Registrada. Bantam Books, 1540 Broadway, New York, New York 10036.***

***PRINTED IN THE UNITED STATES OF AMERICA***

*OPM 0 9 8 7*

## THE GHOSTWRITER TEAM MEMBERS STARRING IN THIS BOOK ARE . . .

Jamal Jenkins

Lenni Frazier

Ghostwriter

Alex Fernandez

Gaby Fernandez

_ _ _ _ _ _ _ _ _ _ _ _

## GADGET DETECTIVE KIT

Here's everything you need for your on-the-go investigations. From pens to notebooks to fingerprint powder and clue-catching tweezers, our kit doesn't leave out a thing!

Check off each item as you put your detective kit together. Then check out the name that's hidden on these pages. Just circle the boldface letters you find in each item on the checklist. Write those letters, in the order they appear, in the blank spaces at the top of the page.

We circled the first one to get you started.

***Detective Kit Checklist***

____ Magnifying (**g**)lass for making small clues appear bigger

| | | |
|---|---|---|
| ____ | Flashlig**h**t | for looking under counters and in dark corners |
| ____ | N**o**tebook and pen | for writing down clues and facts |
| ____ | Envelope**s** and bags | for collecting clues |
| ____ | **T**ape measure | for measuring distances |
| ____ | T**w**eezers | for picking up small clues, such as hairs and threads |
| ____ | A**r**tist's small paintbrush | for brushing on fingerprint powder |

| | | |
|---|---|---|
| ____ | Lead pencil and sandpaper | for making dark fingerprint powder |
| ____ | Talcum powder | for making light fingerprint powder |
| ____ | Roll of clear tape | for taping over fingerprints |
| ____ | Scissors | for cutting the tape you use to pick up fingerprints |

*You'll find out more about fingerprints on page 52.*

## JAMAL'S SECRET CODE JOKES

Knowing secret codes can be important when you're solving a case. On the Ghostwriter team we often have to decode secret messages. Also, I like to send coded messages to Alex. He's a real code nut. Here's one of my favorites, the Tic-Tac-Toe code! Use it to find the answers to the jokes on the next page.

Here's how to make it:

1. Draw three tic-tac-toe boards. Leave one blank. Put dots in the other two boards, as you see in the picture.

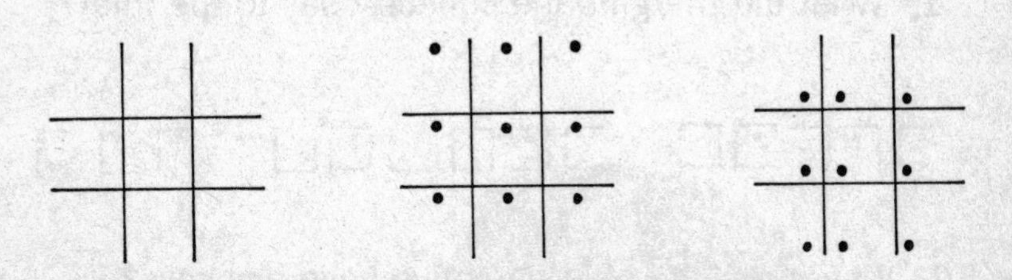

2. Write the letters of the alphabet like this:

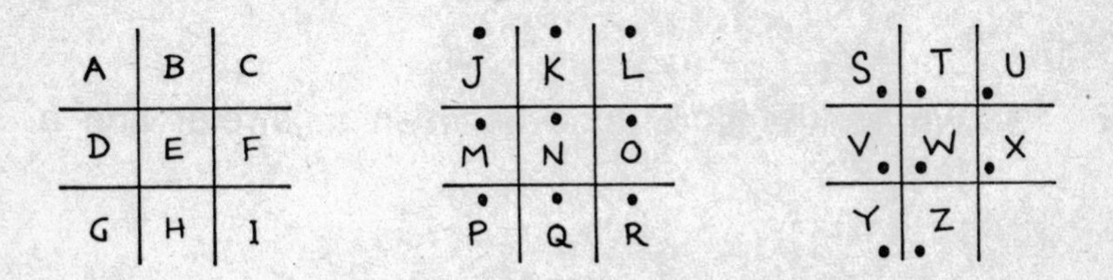


3. The patterns of lines or lines and dots now stand for the letters in the alphabet. Here's how my name looks in the Tic-Tac-Toe code:

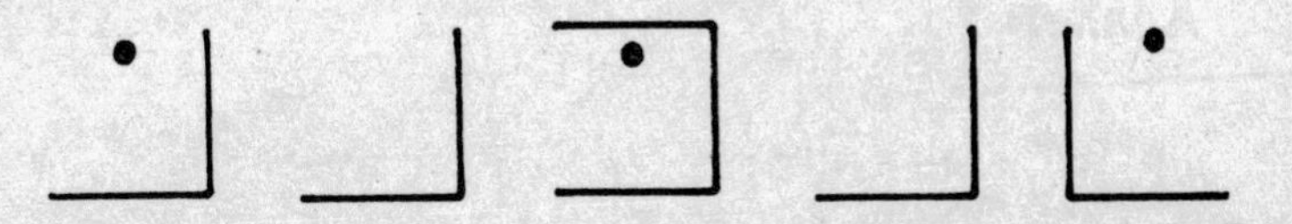

Write your name in Tic-Tac-Toe code here:

______________________________________________

Now figure out the answers to my Tic-Tac-Totally secret jokes!

1. What did the garbage collector say to the thief?

2. Why didn't the bald detective have any keys?

   **Because he didn't have any**

3. What's the difference between a jeweler and a jailer?

   **A jeweler**

   **A jailer**

# GABY'S GHOSTWRITER DECODER WHEEL

There's no getting around it! You'll need a decoder wheel to decipher the message that Ghostwriter left you on the next page. So here's how to put your decoder wheel together—and how to use it!

**What You Need:**

- Scissors
- Alphabet and Code wheels on page 85
- Thumbtack or paper fastener

**What to Do:**

1. Cut out the big Alphabet Wheel and the small Code Wheel on page 85.
2. Put the Code Wheel on top of the Alphabet Wheel, as you see in the picture.

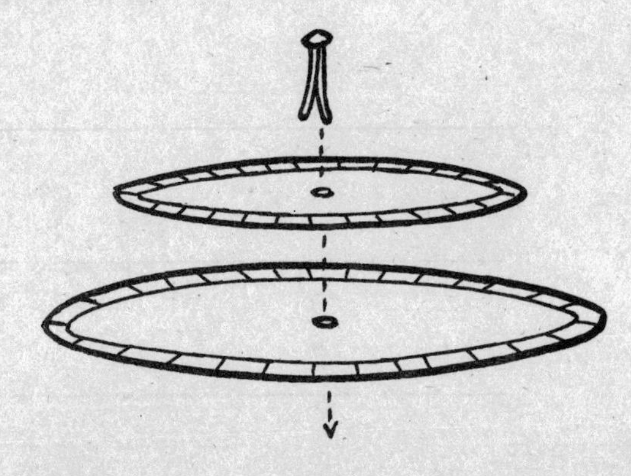

3. Push the thumbtack or paper fastener through the center dots of the wheels. Bend the tabs of the fastener to hold the wheels in place.

**How to Use Your Decoder Wheel:**

1. Ghostwriter's message below is written in Code G. This means that A = G. Turn the small wheel so that the letter *G* is under the letter *A* on the big wheel.
2. Find each letter in Ghostwriter's message on the small wheel. Write down the letter it lines up with on the big wheel.

**Message:** **Znkxk'y g ykixkz skyygmk ot znoy huuq. Nuc corr eua lotj oz? Cnkxk ynuarj eua ruuq? Xkgj zu znk ktj. Zngz'y se irak. Znkt eua'rr qtuc payz cngz zu ju.**

**Translation:** ______________________________

______________________________

______________________________

______________________________

3. To write a message in code, find each letter of your message on the big wheel. Write down the letter it lines up with on the small wheel.

Write a secret message to a friend using Code F!

## MY STERIO USSEC RETMES SAGES

Do you know what the above title says? You will, once I show you my favorite secret codes.

1. **Split It**

This is one of my best codes. It's easy to do, and it always stumps people who don't know how to crack it. Just write down a sentence. Then split the letters so that each word looks completely different.

If you split . . .
**Where was the detective when the lights went out?**
. . . it would look like this:
**Whe rew as thede tect ivew hent heligh tswen tout?**

Now read the answer to my next joke using the **Split It** code.

Answer

2. **Switch It**

This is also a great code. Just switch the last letter of each word with the first letter of the next word.

If you switch . . .
**Where was the detective when the lights went out?**
. . . it would look like this:
**Wherw eat shd eetectivw ehet nhl eightw seno tut?**

Now read the answer to my sister Gaby's joke using the **Switch It** code.

---

Answer

3. **Spin It**

This is my old standby code. All you have to do is spell each sentence backward.

If you spin . . .

**Where was the detective when the lights went out?**

. . . it would look like this:

**Tuo tnew sthgil eht nehw evitceted eht saw erehw?**

Use the **Spin It** code to read the answer.

Krad eht ni.

Answer

4. **Split It? Switch It? Spin It?**

Now figure out which code to use to read: **My sterio ussec retmes sages!**

# LENNI'S LINES

I'm here to show you my lineup of secret codes. All you need to make them are some long, thin strips of paper, a pencil, a pen, and a piece of string.

## 1. **Strip It**

Mark 26 spaces on a strip of paper. Then write the letters of the alphabet, one letter in each space. This is your Alphabet Strip. On another strip of paper, mark 52 spaces and write the alphabet twice. This is your Code Strip.

Alphabet Strip

| A | B | C | D | E | F | G | H | I | J | K | L | M | N | O | P | Q | R | S | T | U | V | W | X | Y | Z |
|---|---|---|---|---|---|---|---|---|---|---|---|---|---|---|---|---|---|---|---|---|---|---|---|---|---|

Now you're ready to use the **Strip It** decoder.
Write your best friend's name here:

________________________________________

Now write his or her name in Code X.

________________________________________

Code Strip

A B C D E F G H I J K L M N O P Q R S T U V W X Y Z A B C D E F G H I J K L M N O P Q R S T U V W X Y Z

Here's how: Slide the *A* in the Alphabet Strip over the first *X* in the Code Strip. Find each letter of your friend's name on the Alphabet Strip. Write down the letter it lines up with on the Code Strip. That's all there is to it!

2. **Wrap It**

Take a strip of paper. Tape one end of the strip to one end of a pencil. Wrap the strip around the pencil tightly and tape the other end. Write your secret message on the strip of paper. Unroll the paper. Your message will be scrambled. When your friends rewrap the paper strip around their pencils, your message will reappear. Try it!

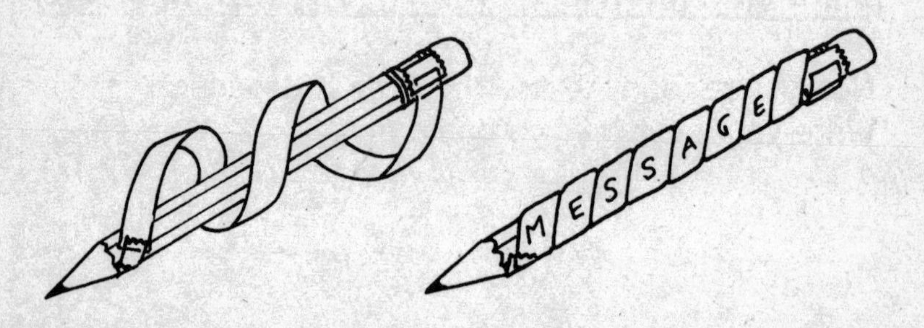


3. **String It**

Trace the letters on the alphabet strip on the next page. Hold a piece of string along the strip, as you see in the picture. Make a dot with a pen at the tip of the string. Next make a dot at the first letter of your message. For example, if your first word is *secret*, make a dot at the *S*. Move this dot to Start, and make another dot above the *E*. Now move this dot to Start before you make the next dot above the *C*.

Trace the alphabet strip below again and give it to a friend. Then you can write secret messages to each other in my **String It** code!

A B C D E F G H I J K L M N O P Q R S T U V W X Y Z

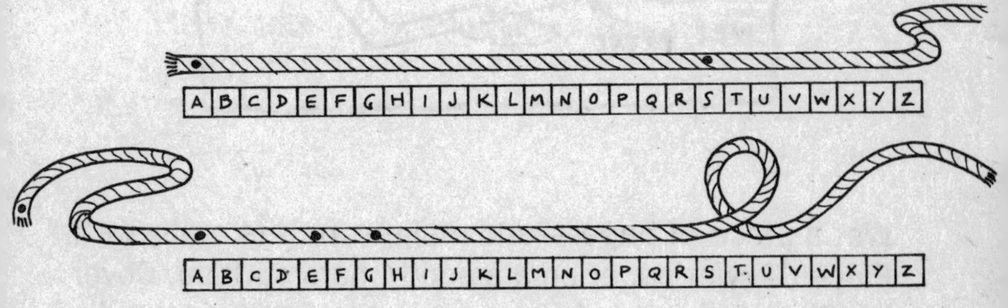


## THINK AGAIN

What do you do when you really want to keep a secret message a secret? Make it invisible! Write it on the back of a letter. Or write it in the blank spaces between the lines. Otherwise, someone might get suspicious when he or she sees you reading a blank piece of paper!

Here are two different ways to make your messages invisible.

1. **Write with Water**

Wet a piece of paper—and make sure it is really wet! Place the wet paper on a smooth, hard surface. Cover it with a dry piece of paper and write firmly on the dry paper with a toothpick. If you hold the wet paper up to the light, you will see your message on it. It will disappear when the paper dries and reappear when it's wet again.

2. **Use a Candle**

Wax a piece of paper by rubbing it with a white candle. Place the waxed side down on a blank piece of paper. Using a toothpick, write your message firmly so that the wax is transferred to the blank paper.

To read your message, sprinkle the paper with black pepper. Shake the paper gently. Pepper powder will stick to the wax and you'll see your message.

**Split It! Switch It! Spin It!** Use one of Alex's secret codes to read the message above.

## TRAPDOOR AND MORE

Sometimes a detective has to set a trap to catch a suspect. Here are three tricks to force someone to leave a clue that he or she was there.

### A little thread . . .

Tape a piece of thread across a doorway. When someone walks through, he or she will break the thread. You can also use a toothpick: As you leave the room, close the door on the toothpick. If someone opens the door while you are out, you will find the toothpick on the floor when you return.

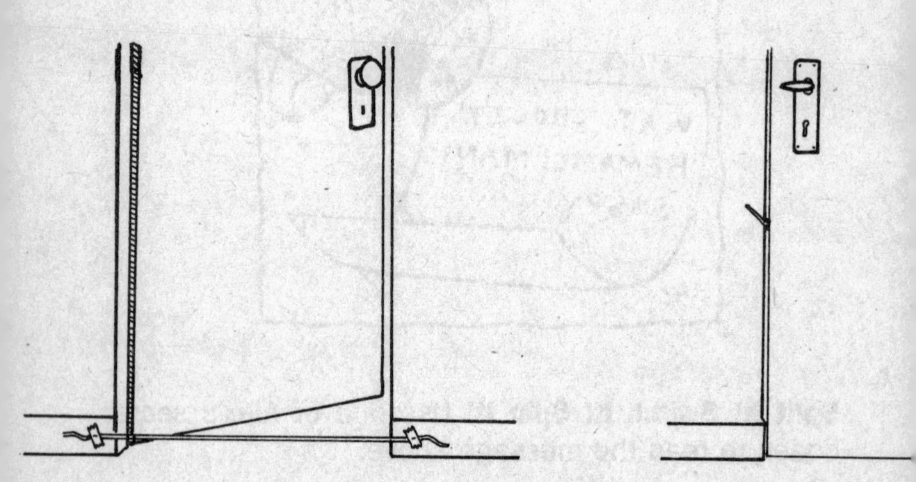

**A piece of hair . . .**

Glue a strand of hair across the opening crack of a drawer or door. If the door or drawer is opened, the hair will come unglued.

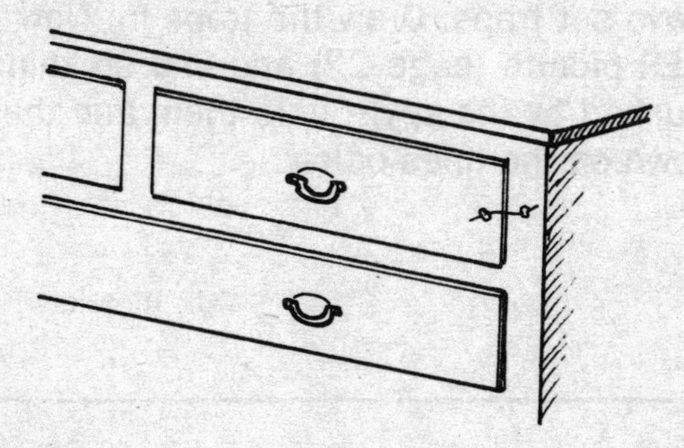

**A tiny mark . . .**

Draw a tiny line that runs across two pieces of paper. Chances are, if the papers are moved, the line will be broken.

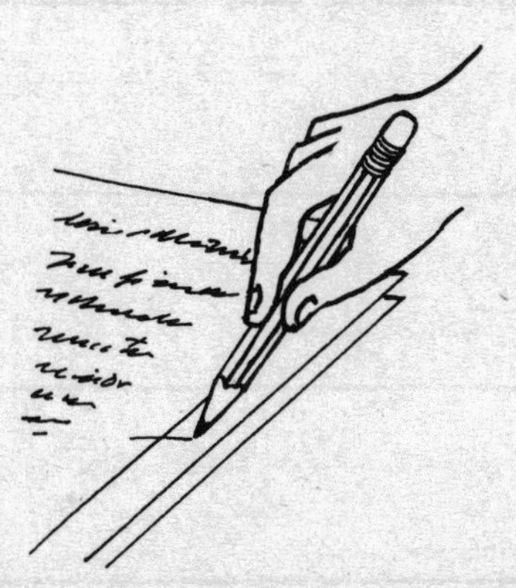

## JAMAL'S ROOM—BEFORE AND AFTER!

Oh, no! Someone's been snooping in my room. Look at the BEFORE picture and find three places where I could have set traps. Draw the traps in. Now look at the AFTER picture (page 22) and find six things that were touched by the spy! Circle them and then write them down on the lines below.

1. ______________________________

2. ______________________________

3. ______________________________

4. ______________________________

5. ______________________________

6. ______________________________

BEFORE
A=B
PHYSICAL FITNESS AWARD
ZPVUI DFOUFS
MAY
A B C D E F G H I J K L M N O P Q R S T U V W X Y Z
THREAD

# AFTER

A=B
PHYSICAL FITNESS AWARD
ZPVUI DFOUFS
B D E F G O T C H A I J K L M N P Q R S U V W X Y Z
MARCH
THREAD
HAIR
PENCIL
E
L
N
A Y F
N
E

## GABY'S SHADOW POWER

What do you do when you're spotted shadowing a suspect? It's time for a quick change! What do I mean? You'll see—just keep reading. Shadow power is all about changing the way you look!

Start out with these quick disguises.

1. **Become a one-armed detective . . .**

Put your arm in a sling. Or take one arm out of the sleeve of your coat. Tuck the empty sleeve into your coat pocket. If you're spotted, take off the sling! Put your arm back into your sleeve!

2. **Change your walk . . .**

There are all kinds of walking styles. Some people walk with tiny steps. Other people glide. And still other people take big, bouncy steps. One great way to disguise yourself is to change the way you walk. You'll be surprised at how much it changes the way you look! And get this: You don't need any props, like slings. All you need is your eyes—and your imagination!

Go outside and watch people as they walk by. Take notes on what you see. Then try to imitate some of the walks you saw. If you're imitating a person who takes small steps, imagine you have a rope around your knees that stops you from stepping out. If you're imitating a person with a bouncy walk, imagine you have balloons tied to your shoulders pulling you up.

Use your disguises along with big hats, colorful scarves, and sunglasses! Put them on and take them off for *Shadow Power*!

## THE MARATHON MYSTERY MESSAGE

*It was a beautiful sunny day in November and everyone was excited about the Big Bike Marathon. Millions . . . no, maybe thousands . . . well, hundreds of bikers were racing. There were exactly 192 more than last year! Best of all, the halfway point was right on my street! You know I was watching—along with Tina, Alex, Lenni, and Jamal. We thought we'd just be there to cheer the bikers on. And I thought I might find a new story for* GabNews, *my newspaper. There are hundreds . . . no, thousands . . . maybe millions of stories in Brooklyn just waiting to be told. And maybe I'd even be on the news. All of the local TV stations would be there covering the race. You see, you never know what's going to happen. We sure didn't know we'd be the ones to save the race!*

—from Gaby's journal

"Here they come!" Alex said, looking far down the street. "I heard some of the racers were fighting on TV this morning."

"Everybody knows how Ace Chasen hates last year's winner, Winnie Slocum," Tina said as she fiddled with her video camera.

"Winnie 'Win'!" Gaby cheered. "She's so cool."

"Ace said Win cheated her out of first place last year by giving her a flat tire," Tina said. "Do you think it's true?"

"Win Slocum would never cheat!" Gaby protested.

"Well, Ace says that Win Slocum won't even finish the race this year," Alex said.

"Well, then, it looks like she's wrong," Jamal said. He pointed. "That's Win Slocum in the lead!"

The bikes were whizzing toward Gaby and her friends. Everyone recognized Winnie Slocum's bright yellow unitard. Lenni started cheering, and soon people in the crowd joined in. Gaby heard cheers in at least six different languages.

Pedaling behind Winnie was Ace Chasen, who was dressed in black. She looked tired. Behind them both was a girl on a silver racing bike. She wore a pink unitard, and her face was bright red under her black helmet. "I don't think she'll be in this race much longer," Gaby told everyone. "A red face is a sure sign of exhaustion."

Right then a person in a baggy trench coat and a rain hat stepped out of the crowd. "That's weird," Lenni said to Gaby. "It's a warm day. No need for a coat and a hat."

The oddly dressed person reached into a pocket, pulled something out, lit it, and tossed it into the street. Flashes and bangs filled the race course.

"Firecrackers!" Alex cried. "Look out!"

The firecrackers were going off right in front of Winnie Slocum's bike. She tried to swerve and another biker crashed into her. They went down together, and more racers piled into them.

Jamal winced. "Ow! What a mess."

"I'm going to help," Alex said. He ran toward the piled-up bikers. Jamal and Lenni went with him.

"Winnie's down!" Gaby cried. "I think she's hurt."

"Uh-huh," Tina said, her eye glued to the viewfinder of her video camera. "This'll be great!" She zoomed in on the big crash scene. "Maybe one of the local news stations will show this tape!"

"I doubt it," Gaby said, standing on tiptoes to peer across the crowd. "I see camera crews from all of the stations right here."

Since Gaby was shorter than most of the people around her, she couldn't see much of what was being done to help the crashed bikers. But she did see something strange across the street. The third-place racer, the one on the silver bike, was pulling out of a dark alleyway. She looked a lot better than she had a few minutes ago.

The crowd broke up as people helped the hurt bikers move to the sidelines. Winnie Slocum limped over to a lamppost and leaned her bike against it. Those who weren't hurt climbed back onto their bikes and continued the race. This time Ace Chasen was in the lead.

Lenni and Jamal came back. The police had asked Alex to be a witness. He was still at the crash site talking to a police officer.

"This race is turning out to be more exciting than I expected!" Lenni said. Jamal was quickly scribbling a description of the scene on his notepad.

"What are the rules of the race?" Gaby asked Jamal. "Is it okay for someone to leave the route? You know, not go very far but sort of go off course?"

"What are you talking about?" he said.

"I saw one of the racers come out of that alley across the street. Why would someone go down there when everyone is going that way?" Gaby pointed down the street.

"Maybe you saw it wrong," Lenni suggested. She led the way down the street.

As they passed Lee DeNoto's Bowling Alley, Gaby saw that the words on the sign had been changed to:

**GO IN ALLEY  SEE NOTE**

"That's a message from Ghostwriter," Gaby whispered to Jamal.

"Well, we'd better go check it out," he said.

They crossed the street, just in time to see a person in a trench coat and a floppy rain hat come running out of the alley.

"Hey," Lenni said. "Wasn't that the person who threw—?"

Before she could finish the sentence, the figure disappeared into the crowd.

The team headed into the alley. There wasn't anything there. No flat bike tires. No empty water bottles. Not one sign of a biker stopping to fix anything.

Lenni was already turning to leave when Gaby spotted a crumpled piece of paper on the ground. She picked the paper up and spread it out. It was a note!

But what did it say? The message made no sense.

**HIT WIN! HEREWES WITCH TOW IN THER ACE.**

"I don't get it," Gaby said.

Lenni read over her shoulder. "It must be a secret message."

Jamal got out his notepad and wrote the message down. He read it three times but still couldn't come up with anything. Then he wrote "Ghostwriter, please show us only the real words."

Ghostwriter went to work. The words on the pad swirled into two lines, like this:

**HIT WIN WITCH TOW IN ACE**
**HEREWES THER**

Jamal showed the pad to Lenni.

" 'Hit win witch tow in ace'? That still doesn't make any sense," Lenni complained.

"Try writing it backward," Jamal wrote, and the words appeared like this:

**ECA REHT NI WOT HCTIW SEWEREH !NIW TIH.**

"That didn't work either," Jamal muttered.

"Too bad Alex isn't here. He's the king of codes," Gaby said.

"Mix them up," Jamal wrote to Ghostwriter.

But no matter how the words were placed, they didn't make a real message.

"Well, it must be from somebody named Ace," Lenni said. "Ace Chasen, maybe?" Her eyes widened. "And it says to 'Hit Win.' That could mean Winnie Slocum!"

Tina gasped. "And now Winnie is out of the race," she said. "I have film of her crashing. If Ace can stay at the front of the pack, she'll probably win."

"That won't be easy," Jamal said. "There's still a long way to go. The finish line is in Central Park."

"Whew!" Gaby exclaimed. "If I pedaled that long, my legs would fall off. It's five and a half miles from here to Central Park."

"How do you know that?" Jamal asked. Then he waved his hand. "Forget I asked. Anyway, these bikers work for months. They practice pacing themselves."

Gaby thought of the red-faced racer on the silver bike. She hadn't looked as if she'd been pacing herself. She'd looked as if she'd already used up every bit of her strength.

"Let's go to my house and catch the winners on TV." Tina said. "Then we can see my tape of the crash."

As the others left the alley, Jamal hung back. He wrote a quick note that said, "Alex, meet us at Tina's." He watched as Ghostwriter swirled the letters around. Jamal smiled. He knew Ghostwriter would make sure Alex got the message. "Thanks," he whispered, even though he knew Ghostwriter couldn't hear him.

When they got to Tina's, she put on the TV while Gaby and the others made popcorn. Alex showed up just as Tina was yelling, "Guys! Come on! Here's the end of the race!"

The team rushed into the living room just in time to see the winner roll across the finish line.

"It's the girl on the silver bike!" Gaby shouted. "The one I saw coming out of the alley." She couldn't mistake that bike.

The crowd on TV cheered. Race officials surrounded the winner as she got off her bike. As the TV sportscaster made his way toward her, a voice-over announced the news.

"And the winner of the Big Bike Marathon is Sonya Simms."

On the screen Sonya Simms smiled and waved, acting just the way you'd expect a winner to act. She looked beautiful, not even half as sweaty and tired as Ace Chasen, the second-place racer.

"This is the most thrilling day of my life," Sonya said into a microphone. "I'd like to thank all those who made it possible—especially my twin sister, Gwenna."

"That's nice," Gaby said. "Would you ever thank me in public like that, Alex?"

"In your dreams," Alex said, grinning.

"Well, Sonya Simms did win the race," Jamal said. "I guess you couldn't have seen her coming out of the alley, Gaby. I think the judges would have disqualified her for leaving the race."

"I *did* see her," Gaby insisted. "Tina, can we play your tape and see?"

"Sure," Tina said. She took the videotape out of her

camera and put it into the VCR. A moment later they were looking at their block, the firecrackers, and the bike racers piling up. Winnie Slocum went down. Ace Chasen zoomed by. And they saw Sonya Simms, behind everyone, turn her silver racer into the alley.

"Hey, there she goes," Lenni said.

"Now do you believe me?" Gaby asked.

Tina hit the stop button on the VCR. The TV returned to more live coverage of the race, and Tina went into the kitchen to get more popcorn. Gaby followed her then stopped when she saw a newspaper on the kitchen table. It was turned to a page with articles about the race. One of the stories was headlined ACE CHASEN, ORPHAN RACER. She began to read it. It explained how Ace Chasen's entire family had died in a terrible fire. "That's so sad," Gaby murmured.

Frowning, she took the strange note from the alley out of her pocket. She picked up a pencil and began drawing lines between letters. Ghostwriter got the idea, and letters began hopping around as he helped her try to make sense of the note.

Suddenly Gaby saw the hidden message. And she also saw the truth about the race. She wrote a note to Ghostwriter explaining what she suspected.

BY GEORGE, I THINK YOU'VE GOT IT, the ghost wrote back.

Gaby ran back to the living room, waving the note. "I got it!" she crowed. "I got it! I broke the code!"

"It was a message about Ace Chasen trying to win through a dirty trick," Lenni said. "How could it mean anything else?"

On the TV screen a sign had appeared, announcing the first- and second-place winners.

1—SONYA SIMMS
2—ACE CHASEN

Letters began to move around as Ghostwriter sent a message.

ACE HAS NO SIS

"See?" Gaby said, pointing to the screen and waving the note in her hand. "This isn't about dirty tricks. Don't you get it? It's about cheating."

Do you get it? Follow the clues to solve the mystery.

## SOLVE IT YOURSELF

1. Write down the names of the racers who were at the midpoint of the race.
2. Cross out the names of anyone who didn't make it out of the crash and continue in the race.
3. Using one of the codes you've read about in this book, decode the message the Ghostwriter team found.
4. Who is cheating? Write down what you think happened!
5. Turn to page 80 and see if you did solve it yourself!

## FOLLOW THAT . . . ?

Footprints and tire marks can be very important clues to follow when you're looking for someone or something—especially if you've lost sight of him or her. Most people might not notice these tracks, but a detective on the lookout will. Here's what some of them look like.

**Car**

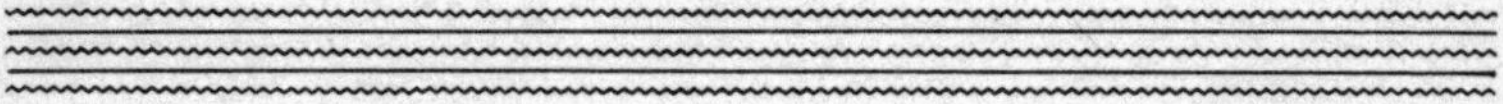

**Truck**

**Bicycle**

**Shoe with heel**

**Shoe without heel**

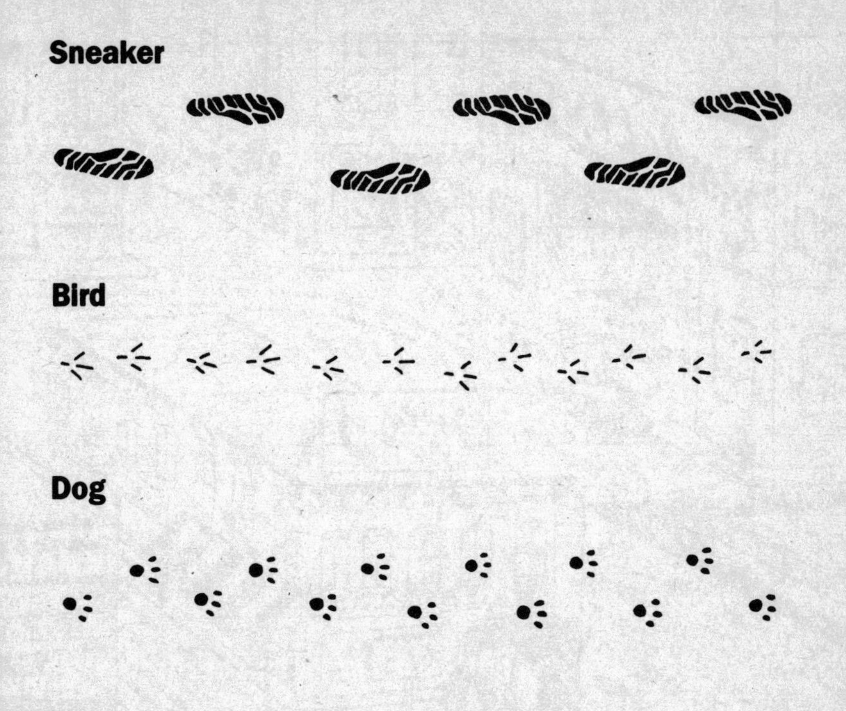


## FOLLOW THAT GRAFFITI ARTIST

Now turn the page and track down a mysterious graffiti artist in our neighborhood.

If you follow the clues he wrote on the building walls, you'll uncover his secret hiding place. Once you think you've found him, hold the page up to the light to see if you're right.

Start at **Lucy's Gas Station**

MOVIELAND
TODAY'S SHOWS
4,6,8 PM
PREMIERE
PARKING
24 HOURS
STOP
U2
LONG LIVE ROCK'N'ROLL
BEST!
COOL
DRUG STOR
GRAND OPENING
POPCORN
THE BEST FRIED CHICKEN IN TOWN
COSMETICS
THE BEST FRIED CHICKEN
GAS
VIDEO MUSI
LUCY'S GAS STATION
I WENT FOR A DRIVE IN A CAR OR A TRUCK. CHOOSE SOME TRACKS AND TRY YOUR LUCK! CLUE: IF YOU PICK THE WRONG SET, YOU'LL GET WET!
BIKE SHOP
BODEGA
YOU'RE HOT ON MY TRAIL—AND SO IS AN ANIMAL WITH A TAIL. I'VE TAKEN A BIKE FOR A SPIN. PICK THE RIGHT TRACKS TO WIN!
GIVE PEACE A CHANCE
STEREO CASSETTE CD SYSTEMS
TILE · LINOLEUM CARPETS

DRUGSTORE
DEAD END
KIM'S GROCERY STORE
KIM'S GROCERY
ANDREA'S MOVING CO.
ANDREA'S MOVING COMPANY
STOP WAR
NO BOMBS
BANK OF THE CITY
THE BEST DONUTS!!
DONUT HOUSE
FOR RENT CALL 313977
NEW!
SAVE THE EARTH
YOU'RE BARKING UP THE WRONG TREE
A=P
FOR THE BEST CUP OF COFFEE IN TOWN STOP IN AT IWTABP'N ON SOUTH PORTLAND STREET
SHOES
CAMERAS
RRRRRRRA
LOOK AT THE WALL, SAY THE CLUES. FIGURE OUT WHICH ARE MY SHOES. UNCOVER MY HIDING PLACE. LIFT THE LID OFF THIS CASE!
CANDY & ICE CREAM
GALINDO
FOR SALE CALL 769-217
RESPECT
ART

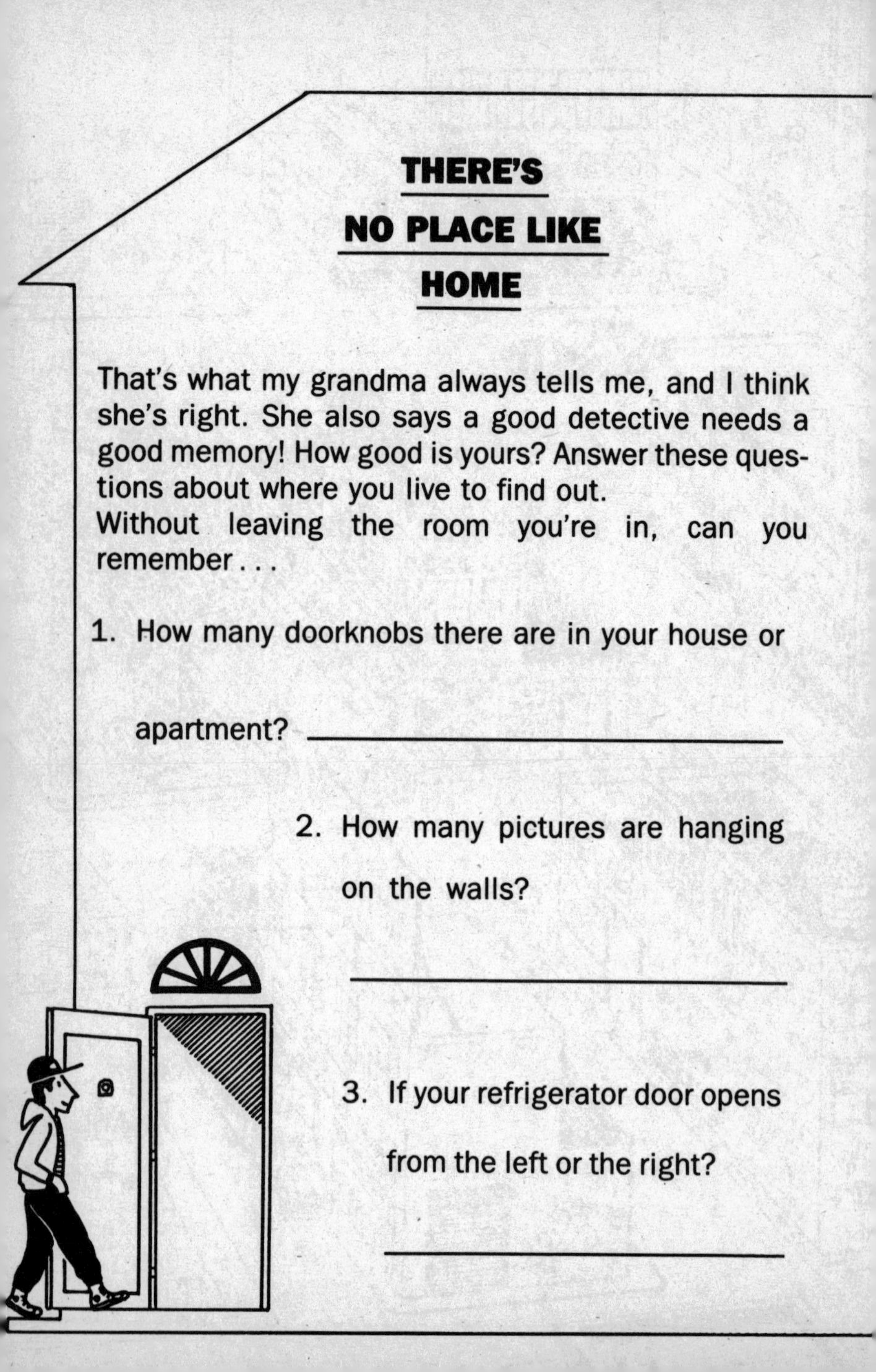

## THERE'S NO PLACE LIKE HOME

That's what my grandma always tells me, and I think she's right. She also says a good detective needs a good memory! How good is yours? Answer these questions about where you live to find out.
Without leaving the room you're in, can you remember . . .

1. How many doorknobs there are in your house or apartment? ________________

2. How many pictures are hanging on the walls? ________________

3. If your refrigerator door opens from the left or the right? ________________

4. How many cabinets there are in your kitchen? ______

5. If the key to your front door turns to the left or right when you unlock the door? ______

6. How many drawers are in the room where you sleep? ______

7. How many pillows are in your house or apartment? ______

8. How many closets and windows? ______

SCORE: Answered all 8? Congratulations, Detective *Homes*!
Answered 6 out of 8? Okay! You've made the *Home* team.
Answered less than 4? Hey! Is anybody home?

## LENNI'S LOGIC

Even though I've never met any of the shoppers in the bodega on the next page, I know who their families are. How? Each shopper has a cart full of *evidence*.

Look in each cart and you'll be able to match the shoppers to their families. Then write down the evidence you found in each cart on the evidence list below!

| EVIDENCE | EVIDENCE | EVIDENCE |
|---|---|---|
| Shopper #1 belongs to family: | Shopper #2 belongs to family: | Shopper #3 belongs to family: |
| **A B C?** | **A B C?** | **A B C?** |
| Circle one. | Circle one. | Circle one. |
| List evidence: | List evidence: | List evidence: |

BODEGA
MUTANT MONSTER CEREAL
FOR A FRIGHTFULLY GOOD BREAKFAST
BREAD
EGGS
BRAMBLES CORNY FAMILY
SOUP
SHAMPOO FOR WHIRLY CURLY GIRLIE HAIR
DAMPERS BABY DIAPERS
PUPPY CHOW
SWEETIE PIE
GRAND OPENING ON SOUTH PORTLAND
COOKIES
VMZI'N WVFZMT
1
A=V
2
BRAN CEREAL
BOOST
HEART-LEE DOG TREAT FOR YOUR FAVORITE PET
BRAMBLES CORNY SOUP FOR ONE
BREAD
EGGS
3
MILLIYUMS CEREAL FOR GREAT BIG FAMILIES
GNAWSOME DOG NUGGETS
BIG CHOW FOR YOUR BIG CHAMP
SHAMPOO
EGGS
BREAD

A

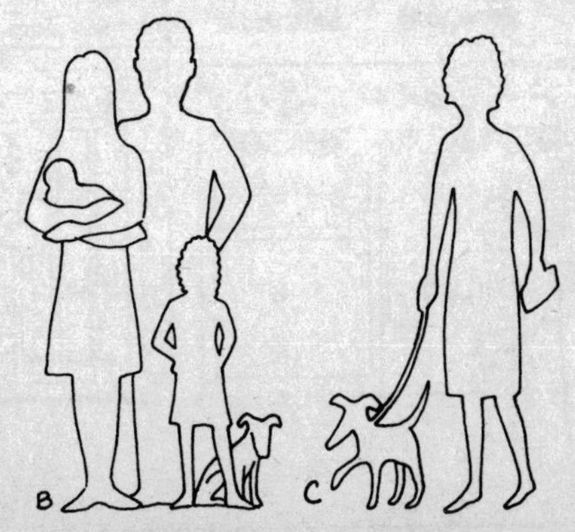
B
C

## WHERE'S WINSTON?

Mr. Braithwaite, our neighbor, has lost his dog. Can you help us find him by following these *clues*?

*Which store is Winston hiding in?*
*Read each sweet clue below.*
*Chew over all the facts you see,*
*And then we're sure you'll know . . .*

*Which dog is Winston!*

**CLUES**

1. Look for a woman eating a vanilla ice cream cone.
2. She is next to a girl who is eating a doughnut.
3. This girl is next to a man who is munching on a cookie.
4. He is also holding a lollipop.
5. Winston is hiding in the store behind this group of people!

Winston is hiding in ______________________

# THE CASE OF THE SHOCKING-PINK ENVELOPE

*Grandma's out of the house each day delivering mail. But I know where I can find her if I need her. I just go to the Fernandezes' bodega between 12:00 and 12:30. She'll be there for her lunch break, a coffee cup in one hand and her mail cart right beside her.*

*I went to find Grandma today because I couldn't figure out how to tell Dad I didn't want to go fishing with him next week. I really like hanging with my dad, but I really hate fishing. It's so slow! Also, I kind of feel sorry for the fish, flapping around on the bottom of the boat trying to escape. One time I helped them. Dad wasn't very happy.*

*Anyway, when I got to the bodega, Grandma was having lunch with her friend Mr. Braithwaite. Mike Edels, the delivery boy, and Mr. Fernandez were there too. So was Alex. I started talking to him about going to Lenni's birthday party that afternoon.*

*All in all, it seemed like a normal day. Who would have guessed that my visit to the bodega would send me on a fishing trip. Fishing for a thief, that is!*

—from Jamal's journal

"Lenni always gets great presents," Alex said. "Remember last year? Her aunt sent her a brand-new fifty-dollar bill."

"Right," Jamal agreed. "She sends Lenni money every year—always in a bright pink envelope." He laughed. "And she always tells her to put it in the bank for a rainy day."

Just then Willie Boylan stepped from behind a stack of cans carrying some dog food. Willie was a big, husky fourteen-year-old who wasn't known for being nice. "Quit blocking the way!" he growled.

He was so busy pushing past the boys that he didn't notice Grandma Jenkins's mail cart. "Yow!" he yelled as he stumbled over it, bumping into Jamal's grandmother.

Grandma Jenkins fell one way. Her coffee cup flew another way. And her mail cart tipped over and fell in a third direction, knocking over the cupcake rack. Mr. Braithwaite's dog Winston barked and lunged for the spilled cupcakes.

"Hey, Winston! Ho, dog!" called Mr. Braithwaite. But by the time he got that big dog under control, cupcakes and envelopes were scattered all around the store.

Alex and Jamal tried to help his grandmother up. "I think I hurt my ankle," she said. Mr. Fernandez and Mike Edels came out from behind the counter to help them.

Mike picked up the cupcake rack and put it back in place. Then he started picking up the scattered mail. While Mr. Fernandez, Alex, and Jamal checked out Grandma's ankle, Willie stood around complaining. "Hey, I'm ready to pay!" he said.

"How about less griping and more help," Alex muttered.

Mr. Fernandez looked at Willie. "You should also apologize to Mrs. Jenkins," he suggested.

"Okay, okay, sorry." Willie picked up some cupcakes and put them back on the rack. But he was doing it wrong. He put pink strawberry cupcakes beside yellow lemon cupcakes. Jamal didn't get it. Anybody could see that the yellow cupcakes should be in one section and the pink ones in another.

"If you're going to stack those cupcakes, please do it right." Mr. Fernandez sounded a little annoyed at Willie. "Put the strawberry cupcakes with the other pink ones. The lemon cupcakes go with the other yellow ones."

Willie looked a little nervous as he picked up another package of pink strawberry cupcakes. He fumbled for a second. Then he put it with the yellow ones.

Mr. Fernandez scowled. "Willie, please. Stack them right, or don't do it at all."

"Who cares if they're pink or yellow?" Willie snapped. "They're just stupid cupcakes."

"I'll stack the cupcakes, Mr. Fernandez," Mike said, standing up. He had both hands full of letters, which he put back in Grandma Jenkins's mail pouch. "You can pick up the rest of the mail," he said to Willie.

Just then a stranger walked into the store. "What a mess," he said, kneeling to help pick up envelopes. Jamal noticed he was holding a Brooklyn street map.

"I'm lost," he said. "Can you tell me how to get to Myrtle Avenue?"

Mike gave the man directions as they finished picking up the mail. The stranger thanked him and left.

By then Jamal's grandmother was taking a few careful steps. "Well, my dignity may be a little beat-up, but I think my ankle is all right," she said. She pinched Jamal's cheek. "See you later, baby. I'd better get back to work." She went to the mail cart, then stopped. "Where's Lenni's mail?" she asked. "The Fraziers' loft is the next stop on my route."

She went through every letter in her cart. Then she went through them again. "I had two envelopes in here for Lenni—and one was a special delivery."

"In a bright pink envelope?" Jamal asked.

"Shocking pink," Grandma Jenkins answered, nodding. "But now I can't find it—or the one in the light blue envelope, either." She looked worried. "They must still be on the floor somewhere."

Jamal was about to start looking on the floor when he caught a glimpse of a newspaper that was lying on the checkout counter. The letters on the page were scrambling around.

Jamal nudged Alex, then nodded at the newspaper. "Ghostwriter!" he whispered.

Slowly the letters settled into a message from the ghost. "DARLING LENNI," it said. "ANOTHER YEAR OLDER AND MORE BEAUTIFUL THAN EVER!"

"Whoa," Alex whispered. "Ghostwriter must be

reading those words from one of Lenni's letters. That means they're still here somewhere."

Ghostwriter was making another message. This one said: "DEAR LENNI, HAPPY BIRTHDAY. PUT THIS AWAY FOR A RAINY DAY."

Jamal grabbed a pen. He knew Ghostwriter couldn't see where the letters were, but maybe there was a way to figure it out.

"Ghostwriter," he wrote. "We need to find Lenni's letters. Do you see any other words near the letters?"

There was a pause. Then the letters on the newspaper started moving again. Ghostwriter's new message read: "LIBERTY. IN GOD WE TRUST. 1985."

"What is he talking about?" Alex asked.

Jamal stared at the strange message. Something about it was familiar to him. He knew he'd seen it before somewhere.

Then suddenly he knew where. Grinning, he reached into his pocket and pulled out a quarter. "Look," he said to Alex. He pointed to the words engraved around the picture of George Washington. "'Liberty. In God we trust,'" he read aloud.

"What was that, Jamal?" Grandma Jenkins asked. She, Mr. Fernandez, and Mr. Braithwaite were still searching the bodega for Lenni's two letters.

"Uh, nothing, Grandma," Jamal said quickly. He waited until she had turned away, then he grabbed Alex's arm. "Lenni's letters are near a quarter," he whispered. "Do you know what that means?"

"Yeah," Alex said. He looked worried. "It means

Lenni's letters are in someone's pocket. It means someone stole them."

Jamal nodded. "The question is, who?"

After a while Alex said, "There's something else I don't get. We all know why someone would steal Lenni's pink envelope."

"Because it has all that cash inside," Jamal put in.

"Right," Alex said. "But Ghostwriter says *both* of Lenni's letters are together in someone's pocket. What I want to know is, why did the thief steal both? Why not just take the pink one?"

Alex and Jamal were both stumped. Jamal wrote a quick note filling Ghostwriter in on everything that had happened. Then, hoping that Ghostwriter could help them, he wrote: "What do you think? Why were both letters stolen?"

Some of the letters shifted on the page. "NO IDEA," Ghostwriter wrote back.

Jamal looked around the store. Then, suddenly, he knew. He was staring right at the most important clue—a clue Ghostwriter couldn't find because he could only read things, not see them.

"Mr. Fernandez," Jamal asked, "do you have a dictionary?"

"Yes, I do," Mr. Fernandez said, looking puzzled. "It's on the shelf under the cash register."

Alex reached down and pulled out the dictionary. He handed it to Jamal. Jamal looked up the word *color*. Here's what he found:

**col-or-***n* A hue as contrasted with black, white, or gray.
**col-or-a-tion-***n* 1 a: the state of being colored > b: use or choice of colors
**col-or blind** *adj* 1: unable to see colors 2: unable to tell the difference between colors
**col-or-cast-***n* : a television broadcast in color

Jamal shut the book with a bang. "You can stop looking, Grandma. I know where Lenni's letters are," he said.

Jamal knows who stole the envelopes. Do you? Follow the clues to solve the mystery.

## SOLVE IT YOURSELF

1. Write down the names of everyone who was in the bodega when the mail cart spilled. These are your suspects!
2. Cross out the names of any suspect who did *not* pick up scattered mail.
3. Cross out the suspects who didn't know about Lenni's party and the shocking-pink envelope.
4. Look at the remaining suspects. Why would one of them have to steal both envelopes? *Hint: The clue is in the cupcakes!*
5. Circle the name of the thief. Then write down how you came to your conclusions.
6. Turn to page 80 and see if you did solve it yourself!

## FINGERPRINTS: HANDS ON!

I can show you how to pick up the most handy clues around: fingerprints!

You'll need the paintbrush, lead pencil and sandpaper, talcum powder, roll of tape, and scissors from your Ghostwriter Detective Kit.
First find a print you want to lift. The best places to look for fingerprints are on flat, smooth surfaces, such as walls, glasses, tabletops, car doors, paper, and envelopes. If the print is on a dark surface, you'll need your talcum powder to make it show up. If it's on a light surface, grab your pencil—it's time to make lead powder!

Hold the pencil over a piece of paper. Then run some sandpaper or a nail file over the side of your pencil point. You'll see lead powder fall onto the paper. Pour the powder into a container.

1. **Pour**

Now that you have your fingerprint powder, pour some of it over the print you want to lift. Remember, light powder for dark surfaces and dark powder for light surfaces.

2. **Dust**

Use the paintbrush to dust the powder lightly from side to side over the print. Cover a wide area around the print. Then gently brush the loose powder away from the print.

3. **Press**

Press some clear tape carefully onto the powdered print. Cut the tape. Press the tape firmly over the print, rubbing your fingernail over it. Now you'll see the pattern of the powder on the tape.

4. **Peel**

Peel off the tape carefully, and the print will come up with it. It will show up again when you stick the tape down on a piece of paper. Be sure to use light paper for dark-powdered prints and dark paper for light-powdered ones.

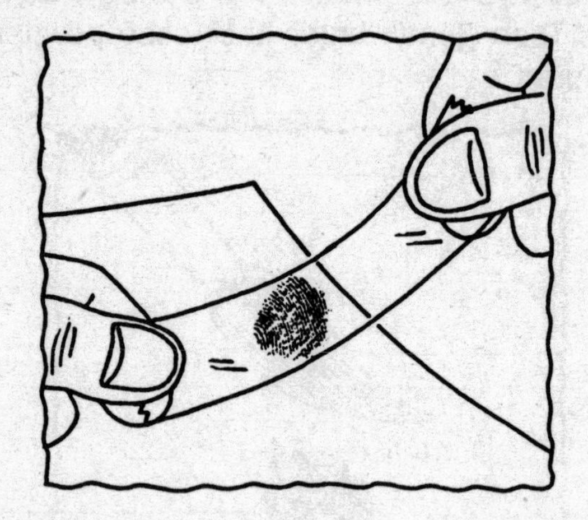

Now you know what it takes to lift fingerprints, and it's as easy to remember as *1 2 3 4*! Write down the four steps here.

1. P ______________________________

2. D ______________________________

3. P ______________________________

4. P ______________________________

## FINGERPRINTS: HANDY GUIDELINES

The lines in fingerprints are a detective's best friend and a crook's worst enemy. So let's put the finger on some facts about these fabulous clues.

As far as anyone knows, no two fingerprints in the world are alike. That's why criminals whose fingerprints are on file with the police department are easy to trace. If they leave prints at the scene of a crime, the police can identify them by checking their files and making a match. Even identical twins have completely different fingerprints. And your fingerprints never change—they stay the same as you grow older.

**There Are Four Types of Fingerprints . . .**

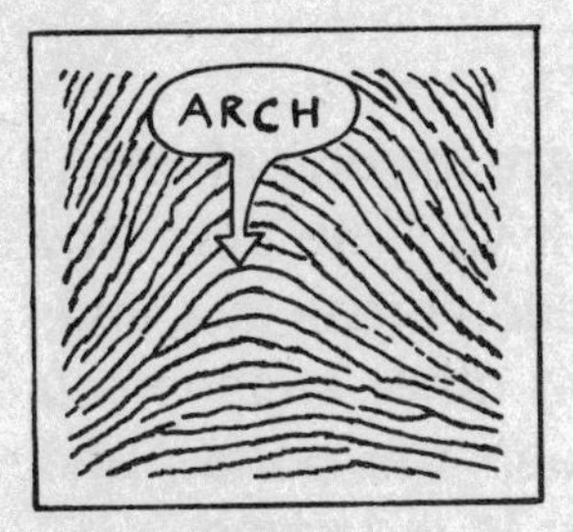


**The Arch**

The shape in the middle looks like an arch.

**The Loop**

The shape in the middle looks like a loop. Whenever you see a loop, you'll find a pattern called a *delta*. The delta is where the loop pattern ends.

**The Whorl**

The shape in the middle is a pattern of lines in a circle. This circle is called a *whorl*. A whorl always has a delta on each side.

**Mixed**

A mixed print is a combination of different types of fingerprints. There are many kinds of mixed prints. One of the most common is the double loop.

**Making a Match . . .**

Decide what type of fingerprint you're looking at: arch, loop, whorl, or mixed. Then see if you can spot any special marks, like a scar or a sudden break in a line. Next, match up the deltas and any other shapes you find. Then count the lines between the deltas and these shapes to see if the number is the same.

**Now match my fingerprint to one of the prints below!**

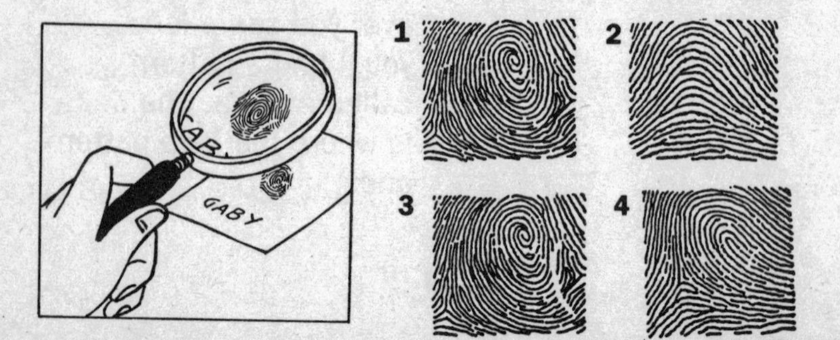

## YOUR FINGERPRINT FILE ALBUM

Keep a fingerprint file. Record your fingerprints right here. Try fingerprinting your friends on a separate piece of paper.

1. Roll the finger you're going to print from side to side on an inkpad.
2. Press the finger very firmly on the paper in this book and roll it from side to side again.

_______________________________________________

YOUR NAME

LEFT HAND

THUMB 1 2 3 4

RIGHT HAND

THUMB 1 2 3 4

---

FRIEND'S NAME

LEFT HAND

THUMB 1 2 3 4

RIGHT HAND

THUMB 1 2 3 4

Now that you've made some prints, you can play . . .

## GABY'S GUESSING GLASS GAME

What You Need:

- Three touchy friends! (Two of them must be in your Fingerprint File Album)
- A drinking glass
- Your detective kit's fingerprint powder, tape, scissors, and magnifying glass

How to Play:

1. Have your friends choose one person from the group. Don't let them tell you who it is! Whoever is chosen should touch the glass and leave a clear print on it—after *you* leave the room.
2. Return to the room. Look for the print with your magnifying glass. Then pour, dust, press, and peel the print off the glass.
3. Press the print down on a piece of paper. Now match it to one of the prints in your album. If you simply can't make a match, then it belongs to the friend you haven't fingerprinted yet!
4. Start again with a clean glass—and ask one of your friends to leave the room and give it a try!

## SEVEN STEPS AT THE SCENE OF THE CRIME

*Whenever I'm at the scene of a crime,*
*I know what to do if I rap this rhyme.*

*1.*
*Look. Don't touch. For good detection,*
*circle the room in one direction.*
*2.*
*Collect fingerprints as you circle again.*
*3.*
*Write in your notebook: Who, Where, and When.*
*4.*
*Gather your evidence. Bag and label each clue.*
*5.*
*Question the victims and witnesses too.*
*6.*
*Look around again for evidence.*
*7.*
*Work out a story: Use common sense.*

Jamal took the pictures on the following pages while we were investigating a break-in at the Party Animal, a party-favor store owned by Mr. and Mrs. Ferguson. The pictures are all mixed up, but you can put them in order by following my rap. I did the first one for you!

What do *you* think happened at the Party Animal? Fill in the blanks to help me work out a story.

Sometime last night on Sunday, December ________,

a crook threw a ____________ through the glass window of the ____________ ____________ at the Party Animal. Then he or she entered. It looked like the crook was someone wearing ____________ from the ____________ I found in the spilled glitter. The crook probably knocked the glitter over when he or she opened the ____________. He or she probably left through the ____________ ____________, as shown by the direction of the ____________ in the glitter.

D
1
EXIT
GFWOSQ
A=S
MONDAY
16
DECEMBER
GLITTER
GLITTER
CLOSED

A

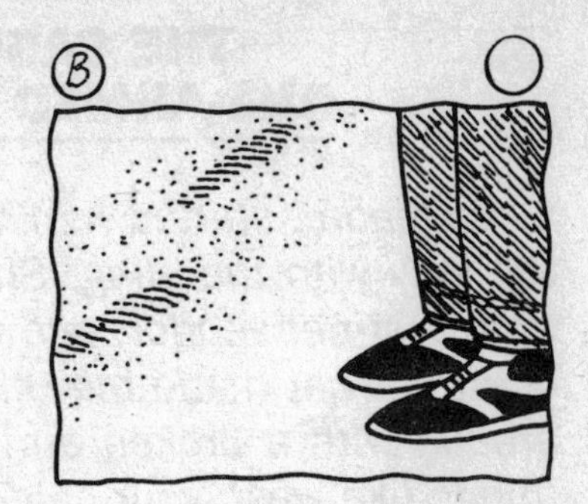
B

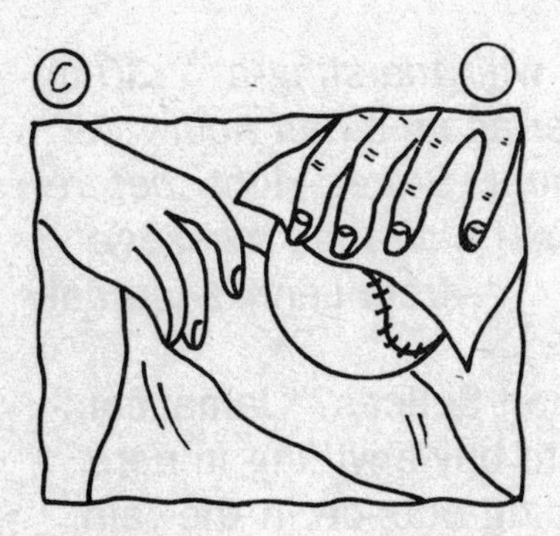
C

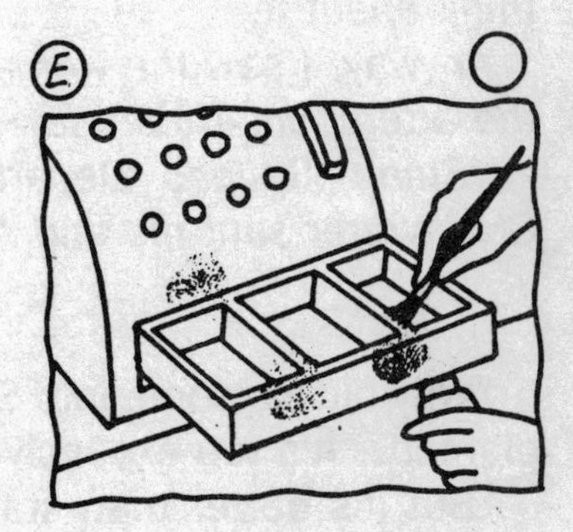
E

F

G
WHO, WHERE,
WHEN

# THE CASE OF THE ONE-ARMED SHOPLIFTER

*If it hadn't started raining, I wouldn't have noticed the lady with the sling. She was buying an umbrella from a street vendor, and the vendor had to help her open it. That made me think. It must be hard to get around with a broken arm. How do you do everyday things like wash your hair? And you couldn't play the keyboard or the guitar. Ugh . . . I don't even want to think about it.*

*Anyway, I saw the woman with the sling at 2:30 in the afternoon. Then I saw her again a half hour later, in Smart Seller's Department Store—right before Ghostwriter sent me and Jamal a strange message!*

—from Lenni's journal

"Why did we come into Smart Seller's?" Jamal complained. "It's too expensive to buy anything in here."

"But it's better than standing outside in the rain," Lenni answered. "Let's go back down on the escalator and see if it's stopped pouring yet."

Lenni leaned over the side of the escalator, trying to look down at all the shoppers on the ground floor. A flash of light by the jewelry counter made her look over at it. There was the woman she had seen outside. She was holding up a beautiful jeweled watch. But something was strange. Outside in the rain her sling had been on her right arm. Now it looked as if she were holding up the watch with her right hand—and the sling was on her left arm.

"Psst!" Lenni hissed to Jamal. "There's something very weird about that woman with the sling! Let's keep an eye on her."

Watching from a moving staircase isn't easy. But Lenni and Jamal tried to observe the lady with the sling. She was talking to a young blond salesgirl at the jewelry counter. She kept holding up the watch and turning it, making the jewels flash.

As they got near the ground floor, Lenni looked up at the message painted over the escalator. It said:

Closing Time: 9:00 P.M.

Suddenly some of the letters began to glow with a golden light. It was a message from Ghostwriter, and it said:

LOSING TIME

"Look!" Jamal whispered. He pointed to the sign.

Lenni read her watch. The time was correct. What did Ghostwriter mean? But she didn't have time to pull out her notebook and ask him. The woman with the sling was walking away!

By the time Lenni and Jamal pushed through the crowd to the jewelry counter, the woman with the sling was nowhere in sight. Lenni looked around for the blond salesclerk, but now there was no one behind the counter. As she stood there, she admired the display of beautiful watches. They were very expensive. Several had diamonds set in place of the numbers.

"Wouldn't one of those be nice to have?" Lenni asked.

"Mine isn't as fancy," Jamal said, showing Lenni the watch on his wrist. "But it still tells the time—it's 3:05 on the dot."

Lenni looked at the fancy watches again and noticed that one box was empty.

"Those are *very* expensive watches," a voice said.

Lenni looked up. It was a saleslady—but not the one she'd seen from the escalator. This saleslady had black hair pulled into a tight bun. She looked disapprovingly at Jamal and Lenni.

"These kids aren't going to buy a watch! How about giving *me* some service here?" a raspy voice said. A big man in a damp black raincoat pushed past Lenni and Jamal. His big black shoes nearly crushed Lenni's feet. The man looked like a prizefighter. He had a nose that had once been broken, and his graying red hair was cut very short in a crewcut. A spicy smell hung around him, like the after-shave Lenni's father wore—one of her favorite smells.

"I just noticed that someone must have bought one," Lenni said. "There's an empty box in there."

"What?" The saleslady peered at the empty box. "I just got here. Let me check the sales slips."

But when she looked at the sales slips, the saleslady gasped loudly. "No, that watch has *not* been sold today! Oh, my goodness!"

"I'm not going to stand around here all day!" the nasty man grumbled. He walked away.

A red-haired saleslady leaned over from the perfume counter next to the watch display. "But, Mr. Gabbe, what about your after-shave lotion?" she called after the nasty man.

But he didn't answer. He just kept walking.

Meanwhile the saleswoman at the jewelry counter was punching a number on the telephone. "You children stay right where you are," she said to Lenni and Jamal in a frightened voice.

"You got it," Lenni said. She had the feeling the saleslady thought she and Jamal might have taken the watch. That bothered her. But even so, she had no intention of going anywhere. Not when it looked like there was a mystery going on.

Luckily, when the manager came over, Lenni recognized him. His name was Mr. Percy. He was a fan of her dad's music. Lenni had seen him at a few of Max Frazier's jazz concerts.

It was a good thing too. Otherwise that nervous saleslady would have had Lenni and Jamal arrested for stealing the watch. The woman was so upset, she couldn't think straight. She even started to cry.

"Oh, Mr. Percy," she moaned. "I feel so horrible. It's all my fault! I broke a heel on the subway. So I stopped off and bought an inexpensive pair of sneakers. Then it started to rain, and . . . and I got here five minutes late. If I had been on time, the watch would never have been stolen! It's all my fault!"

"It's not your fault at all, Jane. We've had a rash of shoplifting lately." Mr. Percy shook his head. "That's the second watch this month. The thief must be a real professional. I don't even know where to begin."

Lenni knew where to begin! She wanted to investigate the scene of the crime as soon as she could. There was a suspect—the lady with the sling—and Lenni wanted to see if she had left any fingerprints. "Uh, Mr. Percy," she began. "Maybe I can help."

After Lenni explained what she had in mind, Mr. Percy gave her and Jamal permission to collect any evidence they could find.

First Lenni looked around the counter at the spot where the woman with the sling had stood. She saw fresh sneaker prints, a strand of red hair, and a damp umbrella. Lenni recognized that umbrella. It was the one the lady with the sling had bought from the vendor.

Lenni got out her fingerprint kit. While she was dusting the glass counter with fingerprint powder, she noticed something else—the smell of perfume in the air. More evidence! Eagerly, she brushed and pressed and peeled off fingerprints. She put the red strand of hair in a small envelope and labeled it.

As she did this, Jamal wrote down all the facts—including "strong perfume in the air." He kept his pen out, ready to question any witnesses.

First Jamal planned to question the nervous saleslady. But when he turned around to ask her his first question, she was gone! When Lenni and Jamal found Mr. Percy, he told them that the woman had gone home, too upset to work.

"Jane has been with us for ten years. She deserves an extra day off," he said.

Lenni asked if they could talk to the other jewelry salesclerk.

"You mean Sally Molter?" Mr. Percy shook his head. "Sal clocked out at three P.M. sharp."

So the young salesgirl's name was Sally. Jamal wrote down, "Question Sally Molter later. Ask if she's ever seen the lady with the sling before today."

Lenni took Jamal's pad to draw a map of the scene of the crime. She labeled the wall behind the counter Mirror. Next to it she wrote "Saw lady with sling here. Sling was on the left arm! Before, it was on her right arm. Very suspicious."

As she finished writing, Jamal spotted Ghostwriter trying to ask them something. The ghost began moving all the letters around in a display sign that said:

What a Bonus! It's a Great Buy!
Real Perfection Perfume

When Ghostwriter was done, it read:

WHAT ABOUT THE REFLECTION?

Lenni stared at the message. Then she got it.

"Of course!" she said. "Reflection! The woman with the sling hadn't changed arms after all. I only *thought* she had, because I had seen her reflection in the mirror."

"Then she's not a suspect?" Jamal asked.

Lenni shook her head. "I don't think so. She still could have stolen the watch."

As they stood by the counter, the smell of all those perfumes was so strong they could hardly think.

"It's a good thing Ghostwriter has some ideas," Jamal said. "Look over there."

Ghostwriter was moving letters around in a sign above some funny-looking perfume bottles. He changed

Toot Sweet! The Hot Perfume in a Horn!
to
TRAP THAT THIEF!

"That's a good idea!" Lenni said to Jamal. "We'll stake out the counter and catch the thief."

When they told Mr. Percy about their plan, he liked it. While Lenni and Jamal hid a few feet away, Mr. Percy pretended to be busy putting up signs that said:

Smart Seller's Year-End Jewelry
Sales! Ladies' Watches—All Styles

Then they waited. But not for long! The lady with the sling came back into the store. Mr. Percy looked up from the jewelry counter and walked to her.

"Oh, no!" Lenni whispered to Jamal. "Doesn't he know anything about trapping crooks? He shouldn't talk to her right away!"

"Hello, dear," the woman said. "I left my new umbrella here."

"Darling!" Mr. Percy answered. "How's your arm?"

"It's Mr. Percy's wife!" Jamal said. "I think you got the wrong suspect, Lenni."

"Here's your umbrella, Mrs. Percy." Lenni handed over the umbrella. As Mrs. Percy took it, Lenni noticed her perfume. It was very light, like spring flowers.

"So much for that trap," she muttered to Jamal.

They waited around a little longer, but nothing happened. Lenni was feeling pretty disappointed as she and Jamal started to leave the store. Then Mr. Percy came running up.

"Another watch is missing!" he said. He looked very upset.

Lenni rushed back to the jewelry counter. Again, she found a strong smell of perfume in the air—and another strand of red hair.

"I'm stumped," she said. "I don't even have a suspect."

Jamal looked just as discouraged. "Maybe we should leave the evidence we found with Mr. Percy," he said.

They went to Mr. Percy's office, but he wasn't there. They sat down to wait for him, and Lenni glanced up at the salesclerks' schedule board on the wall. Here's what she saw:

**SCHEDULE BOARD**

| NAME | Mon. | Tues. | Wed. | Thurs. | Fri. |
|---|---|---|---|---|---|
| *Jewelry Department* | | | | | |
| Ms. Jane Cramer | 3–9 | 3–9 | 3–9 | 3–9 | 3–9 |
| Ms. Sally Molter | 10–3 | 10–3 | 10–3 | 10–3 | 10–3 |
| *Perfume Department* | | | | | |
| Ms. Regina Smith (new trainee) | 10–3 | 10–3 | 10–3 | 10–3 | 10–3 |

Suddenly Lenni had an idea. She copied part of the schedule in her notebook. Then she jumped out of her seat. "Let's go back to the scene of the crime."

She looked around the jewelry counter again and re-listed all of the things they'd found out, making checkmarks beside certain points.

Jamal looked puzzled, but Ghostwriter seemed to understand what Lenni was getting at. Certain letters on the big sale sign began to glow. When Ghostwriter was done, the sign looked like this:

**SM**ART S**ELL**ER'S **Y**EAR-E**N**D J**EW**ELRY
**SALES**! **LAD**IES' WATCHES—ALL ST**Y**LES

Lenni nodded. Ghostwriter was thinking just what she was thinking. "Let's go back to Mr. Percy," she said to Jamal. "We'll ask him to get some people together so we can take their fingerprints. I think I know who the thief is."

When Mr. Percy had gotten everyone together, Lenni took a set of fingerprints from the person she suspected. She compared them to the ones at the counter.

They matched!

"I was right," Lenni told Jamal.

"But how did you figure it out?" Jamal wanted to know.

Lenni grinned. "I just followed my nose!"

Do you know who the thief is? Follow the clues to solve the mystery.

## SOLVE IT YOURSELF

1. Write down the names of everyone who was near the jewelry counter. These are your suspects.
2. Sneaker prints were found near the counter. Who do you *know* was *not* wearing sneakers? Cross out that name.
3. Lenni and Jamal smelled strong perfume at the scene of the crime. Who do we *know* was *not* wearing strong perfume? Cross out that name.
4. A red hair was found at the counter. Cross out the names of any suspects who do not have red hair.
5. Circle the name of the thief. Then write down how you came to your conclusions!
6. Turn to page 84 and see if you did solve it yourself!

## GHOSTWRITER'S SECRET MESSAGE

As Jamal, Lenni, Alex, and Gaby walked through the neighborhood, they spotted something wrong. Some of the signs were missing. But I found them—and you can too. They're hidden in this book!

To find the missing signs:

1. Turn back to the page number written on each building or sign in the picture on the next page.

2.  When you see this symbol, you've found the missing sign. But it's in secret code.

3. Use your decoder wheel to decode the sign, following my clues.

4. Write your answer in the blanks in the picture.

*Now there's only one more thing left for you to do!*

**There's a New Detective I Want on the Team!**

To find out who it is:

1. Circle the first three letters of each sign you just decoded.

2. Now read what you've circled and you'll have the answer!

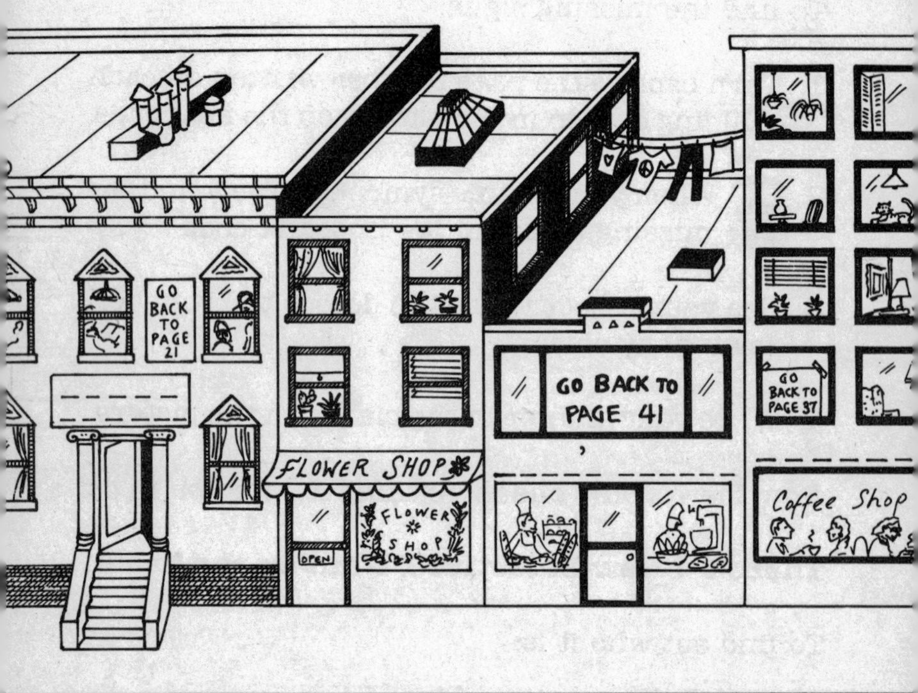
GO BACK TO PAGE 21
FLOWER SHOP
FLOWER SHOP
OPEN
GO BACK TO PAGE 41
GO BACK TO PAGE 37
Coffee Shop

BOOKS & MORE
PARTY·ANIMAL
OPEN
GO BACK TO PAGE 43
GO BACK TO PAGE 62

# ANSWERS

**Pages 2–4**

Ghostwriter

**Page 6**

1. Grime doesn't pay
2. Because he didn't have any locks
3. A jeweler sells watches
   A jailer watches cells

**Page 8**

There's a secret message in this book.
How will you find it? Where should you look?
Read to the end. That's my clue.
Then you'll know just what to do.

**Pages 10–12**

1. They stepped on a scale and got away (a weigh).
2. His nose
3. In the dark.
4. Use the Split It code: Mysterious Secret Messages!

**Page 17**

1. Split It code: Watch out. The mailman is a spy.

A=B
PHYSICAL
ZPVUI
DFOUFS
FITNESS AWARD
MARCH
BDEFGOTCHAIJKLMNPQRSUVWXYZ
THREAD
PENCIL

**Page 32**

1. Ace Chasen
   Winnie Slocum
   Sonya Simms
2. Cross out Winnie Slocum. She left the race after the crash.
3. Use the Split It code: Hi twin! Here we switch to win the race.
4. The rider on the silver bike at the midpoint of the race was Gwenna Simms—Sonya Simms's twin sister. Gwenna and Sonya switched in the alley, and Sonya Simms finished the race. The person in the raincoat who Gaby saw coming out of the alley was Gwenna—after the switch! Sonya Simms cheated to win the race!

**Pages 36–37**

For illustrated answer turn to page 82.

**Pages 40–41**

1-B, 2-C, 3-A

**Page 42–43**

Winston is hiding in Cohen's Ice Cream Store.

**Page 50**

1. Mr. Fernandez
   Mr. Braithwaite
   Jamal
   Grandma Jenkins
   Alex

Mike Edels
Willie Boylan
The stranger
2. Cross out everyone except Willie, Mike, and the stranger. They were the only ones who picked up mail.
3. Cross out the stranger. He walked into the store *after* Jamal and Alex talked about Lenni's birthday party and the shocking-pink envelope.
4. The remaining suspects are Mike Edels and Willie Boylan. Willie would have to take both envelopes because he is colorblind. Remember—he couldn't tell the difference between the pink cupcakes and the yellow ones! Therefore, he wouldn't be able to tell which envelope was the *shocking-pink* one with the money in it.
5. Willie Boylan stole the shocking-pink envelope!

**Pages 56**

Number 3

**Page 61**

Sometime last night on Sunday, December *16*, a crook threw a *baseball* through the glass window of the *front door* at the Party Animal. Then he or she entered. It looked like the crook was someone wearing *sneakers* from the *footprints* I found in the spilled glitter. The crook probably knocked the glitter over

MOVIELAND
TODAY'S SHOWS
4,6,8 PM
PREMIERE
POPCORN
PARKING
24 HOURS
STOP
LONG LIVE ROCK'N'ROLL
BEST!
COOL
DRUG STOR
GRAND OPENING
THE BEST FRIED CHICKEN IN TOWN
COSMETICS
THE BEST FRIED CHICKEN
GAS
VIDEO MUSI
LUCY'S GAS STATION
I WENT FOR A DRIVE IN A CAR OR A TRUCK. CHOOSE SOME TRACKS AND TRY YOUR LUCK! CLUE: IF YOU PICK THE WRONG SET, YOU'LL GET WET!
BIKE SHOP
BODEGA
YOU'RE HOT ON MY TRAIL—AND SO IS AN ANIMAL WITH A TAIL. I'VE TAKEN A BIKE FOR A SPIN. PICK THE RIGHT TRACKS TO WIN!
GIVE PEACE A CHANCE
STEREO CASSETTE CD SYSTEMS DIGITAL
TILE. LINOLEUM CARPETS

UGSTORE
DEAD END
KIM'S GROCERY STORE
KIM'S GROCERY
ANDREA'S MOVING CO.
ANDREA'S MOVING COMPANY
STOP WAR
NO BOMBS
THE CITY
BANK OF
THE BEST DONUTS!!
DONUT HOUSE
FOR RENT
CALL 212477
NEW!
SAVE THE EARTH
YOU'RE BARKING UP THE WRONG TREE
A=P
FOR THE BEST CUP OF COFFEE IN TOWN STOP IN AT IWTABP'H ON SOUTH PORTLAND STREET
SHOES
CAMERAS
FOR SALE
CALL 769-217
RRRRRRR
LOOK AT THE WALL, SAY THE CLUES. FIGURE OUT WHICH ARE MY SHOES. UNCOVER MY HIDING PLACE. LIFT THE LID OFF THIS CASE!
CANDY & ICE CREAM
GALINDO
RESPECT
ART

when he or she opened the *cash register*. He or she probably left through the *back door*, as shown by the direction of the *footprints* in the glitter.

**Pages 62–63**

A-7, B-6, C-4, D-1, E-2, F-5, G-3

**Page 73**

1. Sally Molter
   Mrs. Percy
   Jane Cramer
   Mr. Gabbe
   Regina Smith
2. Mr. Gabbe. He nearly stepped on Lenni's feet with his big black shoes.
3. Mrs. Percy. She was wearing a light perfume, like spring flowers.
4. Cross out Sally Molter and Jane Cramer.
5. The only suspect left is Regina Smith. She works at the *perfume* counter, right next to the jewelry counter. She's a new employee, and she has red hair!

**Pages 76–77**

Page 21: YOUTH CENTER
Page 41: AREN'S BAKERY
Page 37: THELMA'S
Page 43: NEWSSTAND
Page 62: ONE WAY

YOU ARE THE NEW ONE